T0228493

For
my parents,
who would love
me even if I weren't
a super magnificent artist.

Katherine Tegen Books is an imprint of HarperCollins Publishers. Oh, Olive! • Copyright © 2023 by An-Li Cho • All rights reserved. Manufactured in the United States of America. No part of this book may be used or reproduced in any manner whatsoever without written permission except in the case of brief quotations embodied in critical articles and reviews. For information address HarperCollins Children's Books, a division of HarperCollins Publishers, 195 Broadway, New York, NY 10007. www.harpercollinschildrens.com • Library of Congress Control Number: 2022940753 • ISBN 978-0-06-323749-0 • The artist used sumi ink, graphite, gouache, acrylic, and colored pencils to create the illustrations for this book. • Typography by Chelsea C. Donaldson 23 24 25 26 27 PC 10 9 8 7 6 5 4 3 2 ❖ First Edition

OH, OLIVE!

LIAN CHO

KATHERINE TEGEN BOOKS
An Imprint of HarperCollins Publishers

Olive Chen is an artist.

Olive is the most magnificent and brilliant
artist in the whole wide world.

KNOCK KNOCK!

Or so she thought anyway.

Olive's parents were also artists.
Serious artists.

Her father painted squares.

Her mother painted triangles.

They knew that one day Olive
would also paint brilliant squares
or magnificent triangles.
Just like them.
But they didn't know when
it would happen.

From the moment she was born,
they tried their best.
Olive's father showed her pictures.

Olive's mother showed
her blocks.
But Olive wasn't
interested in any shapes.

"Oh, Olive. Artists don't smear. Why don't you draw a square for school tomorrow?"

"Oh, Olive. Artists don't lick. How about a triangle instead?"

No matter how hard they tried, it became clear that Olive just could not paint a shape.

The next morning, Olive went to school.

Olive listened VERY closely to the teacher and painted VERY seriously on her classmates.

By the end of the year, Olive still hadn't painted what anyone asked her to.

Beautiful square, Marco.

Spectacular circle, Rosie.

An amazing triangle, Nadira.

"I don't think you should paint a shape," said Marco.

"I like your paintings just the way they are," said Nadira.

"I wish I knew how to paint like you!" said Rosie.

And the rest of them agreed.

"Anyone can do it," said Olive. "I guess I can show you how . . ."

"Grab some paint and
a paintbrush or two."

"How about blue?"

"YES!"   "Pink?"

"YES!"   "Green?"

"DUH!"

"That's more like it!"

"It's getting there. But
I think we need . . ."

the square house

the triangle house

the walls

the coffee shop

the pet store

Mr. Hooper and his baby

and finally, her parents' art museum . . .

But then Olive's parents looked closer . . .

"Oh, Olive! This is beautiful!"

"Look at all your fabulous colors. You've been a magnificent artist all along."

"I know," said Olive.

"It's okay that you can't paint a shape. Our painting could use some of your brilliant and wacky splatters."
They handed her a paintbrush.
"Why don't you surprise us?"

So Olive did.
 She painted with every color.
  She painted a line there and a stroke there.
   She splashed and she splattered.
    She painted what she felt, what she could paint all along.

Olive painted . . .

the world's most perfect circle.